I WA
THERE

*Always trust
and believe in
Proverbs 16:9*

I WAS THERE
Second Edition
Destined to Witness

GARY G. GABLE

TATE PUBLISHING
AND ENTERPRISES, LLC

I Was There – Second Edition
Copyright © 2015 by Gary G. Gable. All rights reserved.

No part of this publication may be reproduced, stored in a retrieval system or transmitted in any way by any means, electronic, mechanical, photocopy, recording or otherwise without the prior permission of the author except as provided by USA copyright law.

Scripture quotations marked (NIV) are taken from the *Holy Bible, New International Version*®, NIV®. Copyright © 1973, 1978, 1984 by Biblica, Inc.™ Used by permission of Zondervan. All rights reserved worldwide. www.zondervan.com

The opinions expressed by the author are not necessarily those of Tate Publishing, LLC.

Published by Tate Publishing & Enterprises, LLC
127 E. Trade Center Terrace | Mustang, Oklahoma 73064 USA
1.888.361.9473 | www.tatepublishing.com

Tate Publishing is committed to excellence in the publishing industry. The company reflects the philosophy established by the founders, based on Psalm 68:11,
"The Lord gave the word and great was the company of those who published it."

Book design copyright © 2015 by Tate Publishing, LLC. All rights reserved.
Cover design by Allen Jomoc
Interior design by Caypeeline Casas

Published in the United States of America

ISBN: 978-1-68164-949-8
1. Fiction / Short Stories (single author)
2. Fiction / Religious
15.07.10

DEDICATION

To my wife and coworkers in my life whose
God-given purposes crossed with mine.

CONTENTS

Preface 9

Introduction 11

Destiny to Share 15

Destiny to Be Sacrificial 19

Destiny to Be Blessed Sacrificially 23

Destiny to Bear Burdens 26

Destiny to Serve 30

Sequa 37

The Clock Stop Watcher 38

Where Can I Go From Here? 41

Sequa 42

PREFACE

Where do inspiration, insight, understanding, and wisdom come from but through the originator of the Word? Psalm 71:17–18 says it so aptly.

> Since my youth, O God, you have taught me, and to this day I declare your marvelous deeds. Even when I am old and gray, do not forsake me, O God, till I declare your power to the next generation, your might to all who are to come.
>
> (NIV)

Psalm 148: 7-12

Praise the lord from the earth, you great sea creatures and all ocean depths, lightning and hail, snow and clouds, stormy winds that do his bidding, you mountains and all hills, fruit trees and all cedars, wild animals and all cattle, small creatures and flying birds, kings of the earth and all nations, you princes and all rulers on earth, young men and maidens, old men and children.

INTRODUCTION

God comes to individual people in uniquely individual ways. Psalm 46:10 says, "Be still and know that I am God." God reigns in the world he created. He governs every aspect of it from the first time he said, "Let there be..." Matthew 10:29 points out that even a sparrow is noticed when it falls to the ground. He gives food to all mankind, animals, and even plants, whether they know it or not. For anyone who seeks truth must first find the source or revelation of that truth, and that truth comes from the Son, Jesus Christ, sent by God the Father, as revealed in Scripture.

I believe every sane person in this world wants to develop a purpose for their life. I invite the reader to come on a journey of sorts. Part one is a journey that encompasses God's creation which witnessed to His word.

Part two reflects on the question, "Is God's Word still speaking to me today?" "If it is speaking, what does it say?" "What is my purpose in all this?" the reader will have opportunity to search the Word of God. It is very possible that the reader will connect to some experience or event. Then that experience can be explained by the title in the book, "I was there, destined to witness."

I pray the words of Proverbs 16:9 will go hand-in-hand in the reader's life: "In his heart a man plans his course, but the Lord determines his steps." (NIV)

PART ONE

WHEN GOD'S VOICE SPOKE IN THE PAST

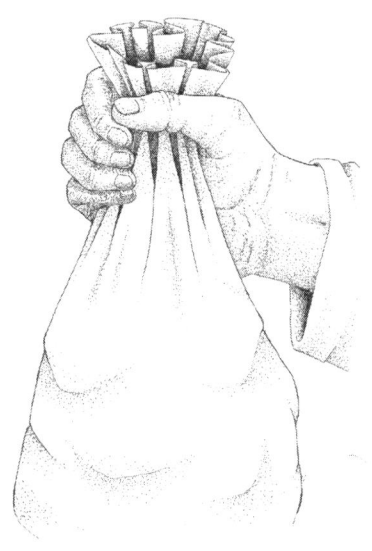

Here is a boy with five small barley loaves and two small fish, but how far will they go among so many?

John 6:9

DESTINY TO SHARE

I was jokingly told by my parents that I was dropped from the sky and landed in their home. After I began to tell my play friends where I came from, my parents felt it was time to tell it to me straight. Regardless, I felt loved and a part of something. Being a boy, I was taught how to take care of my things and learn how to work like my father. My parents sent me to school to learn the Torah. I was expected to become a man in my community, who would one day have a wife and family of my own. (I could then joke that my children fell from the sky.) In the meantime, I had much to learn.

When I was about ten years old or so, I remember hearing my parents talk about a man who had performed some miracles. They said he talked about the kingdom of God, about something new called baptism, and about himself as God's Son. My parents wanted to see him and meet him. They wanted to see for themselves who this prophet was. I became curious too, but I was just a young boy who was curious about a lot of things in life.

Word reached our small town that this prophet, this teacher, named Jesus was near. People said he was going to a hillside next to Lake Galilee. That was close by. The day was just getting started, but my parents stopped what they were planning and told me we were all going as a family right away.

Mother was the prepared type. She often had food ready hours before mealtime. Since we were leaving in a hurry, my mother grabbed some loaves of bread and two small dried fish. This would take care of our family for the day in case we would not get back home until late in the evening. Mother told me to wrap up the food, and we set off to find this Jesus. Already, our neighbors and friends were on the road together with a lot of other people.

As we approached the hillside by the lake, Father said, "Look, there he is." He was sitting on a rock with a small group of men around him also sitting on rocks or on the ground. There was a huge number of people coming up to the hill and sitting and waiting for this Jesus to do or say something. In my enthusiasm, I said to my parents, "I am going up a little closer to see because I cannot see over all these people who are crowding in." Father said, "Be careful and do not disturb those men."

I got really close so I could hear what they were talking about. I could not understand everything they said, but it was something about having enough money for food. I scooted a little closer and leaned in a little, when one of the men noticed me carrying the wrapped food I brought for the day. He beckoned me to come to him and to show the food I had to this Jesus man. He asked Jesus how much of what I had could feed so many. I stood there with my mouth open in awe. This Jesus man took what I had and asked everyone everywhere to sit down.

Jesus held our family's bread, five loaves and two fish, in his hands and prayed. Right before my eyes, the bread and fish were multiplied to become armfuls of bread and

fish to hand out to every last person that came. I looked back to where my parents were in amazement. They had no idea this miracle just happened from the little food we had wrapped for the day. It was right then and there I knew I would follow Jesus. It was not just the food we ate, but his words were powerful, filled with meaning and hope. My life was changed forever from earthly meaning and purpose to a spiritual, heavenly meaning held by promises I was to see come true someday.

Abraham looked up and there in a thicket he saw a ram caught by its horns. He went over and took the ram and sacrificed it as a burnt offering instead of his son.

Genesis 22:13

DESTINY TO BE SACRIFICIAL

I was told by my mother that I began in her. The earliest I can remember is my mother showing me where I could find food. I recall finding food wherever my mother was. I also loved to wander away, but my mother would call me back when she made bleating sounds. Life was good.

As I grew bigger, my mother did not pay much attention to me. I bravely wandered over the fields of grass with my friends in search for food and adventure. During these times, I really became aware that I could go only so far before some creatures stopped us from going any farther. I knew I walked and ran on all of my legs. But what stopped us from going farther were creatures that moved only on two of their legs. They never hurt me or made me scared. Actually, they moved us to food and water, like my mother used to do. Two hard things began growing on my head. My mother said they were called horns so I could protect myself. Life was a good feeling: protected and fed.

After a few seasons had come and gone, I felt urges to go where I never had gone before. Would I find more and better food? Could I find more friends, who like me, moved on all their legs?

On one particularly hot morning, I felt a strong urge to go some place I had never been before. I looked for a place to run away from those two-legged creatures and do some exploring on my own. This seemed easy to me. I walked and waited until I did not see any two-legged creatures. At that moment, I ran as fast as I could over some low hills. It was wonderful. There were bushes, grass, and trees all around me. Happily, I began eating.

I was so focused on food that I did not notice two two-legged creatures coming in my direction. One had a large load of branches on its back. I froze. Did they see me? I could hardly breathe. I moved back and turned to run. I ran straight into a very thick bush. My horns quickly tangled up in the branches and I could not get away. I thought that if I would be really still, those two would go away, and then I would try again to get free.

While I was waiting for my chance to free myself, sounds came from above me, sounds from the sky. When the sounds stopped, there was silence everywhere. It was so quiet I heard thumping in my body. The two-legged creatures were looking right at me. I was stuck with no place to go. The bigger of the two creatures came to where I was. It grabbed my horns and pulled me free! I was so glad to be free! I did not struggle away. I knew from before that these creatures had given me food and water, and I felt safe again. I was lost before and was found stuck while trying to run

I WAS THERE

in my own way of choice. Next, I was gently laid on a pile of branches. I was being taken care of, safe in the creature's care. I fell asleep in the love I knew was there.

Jesus said to them, "Come and have breakfast." None of the disciples dared to ask him, "Who are you?" They knew it was the Lord. Jesus came, took the bread and gave it to them, and did the same with the fish.

John 21:12–13

DESTINY TO BE BLESSED SACRIFICIALLY

I was told by my cluster friends that I began as an egg. My first memories were moving around in something that covered me all over. I moved freely, up and down and back and forth. Other friends in my cluster would move easily past me, over me, and beneath me. Life was happy. I found little pieces of food moving around me. Sometimes, my friends and I would try to get the piece of food from each other. It was not much fun when my friend took away my food just when I had my mouth open to swallow. I always was looking for food.

My world had so many times of light, then dark times. This never stopped. It went on and on: light, dark, light, dark. I even learned the best time between light and dark to search for food. I was growing bigger and bigger and needed more space in which to move. Many of my friends and I glided wherever we wanted and ate all we could find. Life was so happy.

I remember that one time when my friends were in a change from dark to light, everything changed forever.

Suddenly, with a swish-and-whoosh sound, something forced my friends and me to be squeezed right next to each other. This was very uncomfortable, and we had nowhere to go. We pushed back and wiggled, but the more we struggled, the more we were squished together. A big covering wrapped around us. Whatever I had moved in before all my life was gone. We saw strange creatures moving us to a place where we could not find our breath. We fought bravely to try to get free.

Then suddenly, the most wonderful feeling came over me. One of the creatures picked me up. His touch stopped my fighting to be free. There was a new sound I never heard before. It came from the creature holding me. I understood it, "Come and have breakfast." I was totally lost in his care. Whatever struggles I had experienced in the past meant nothing to me now. It felt completely safe to be there. I had a new life all over again in never-ending joy.

I WAS THERE

When they brought the colt to Jesus and threw their cloaks over it, he sat on it.

                Mark 11:7 (Also Matthew 21:6–7)

DESTINY TO BEAR BURDENS

I was told by my mother I came from a loving father and her, who both worked their whole lives. Mother showed me where I could get milk for food. And oh, I loved the sweet smell and taste of fresh hay. I loved growing up. My mother said how proud she was as I was getting big and strong like my father. Little did I realize it, but all the hard work my father was doing was soon to be taught to me.

One of those ways of learning was by a two-legged master. This creature tied me to my mother so I could learn to follow directions. I had not carried anything on my back yet like my mother had to do. I saw how patiently she waited for the orders to stand still, go ahead, turn, and follow wherever she was pulled.

I especially remember one warm day that I had an unexpected first lesson on carrying a load. My mother and I were tied up at our master's house just watching all kinds of two-legged creatures walking in all kinds of directions. That is when it happened. Two two-legged creatures I had never seen before came up to me and untied me to be led away. I was never far from my mother before, and I began to be a little nervous. My master stopped us and made some sounds to the two-legged creatures leading me. My master patted me on my head and back as if to encourage me to go where I was being pulled.

I was led to a new place I had never seen. I remember how gently I was being touched. All of the two-legged creatures were quietly making noises to one of their kind. In a surprise to me, this creature was put on my back after some covering was put on me. Wow! This was my first workload, my first burden, my first assignment. I remember how my mother looked when some of her loads were heavy and she would grunt. But my first experience was not that heavy. Rather, I felt energy and strength while carrying this creature as he touched my neck. I felt so comfortable and assured where he was guiding me.

What began as a quiet walk soon changed. From everywhere came all kinds of two-legged creatures. They made loud noises. They waved clothes and branches and threw them on the ground

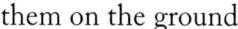

right where I was walking. The gentle hand on my neck gave me calm over my instinct to run away from the noise. As I was guided along, I began to notice the same sounds over and over. I began to understand those sounds as something very special. "Hosanna to the Son of David!" "Blessed is he who comes in the name of the Lord!" "Hosanna in the highest!" Wow! This was special. This creature on me was special! I felt like I was in the middle of a lot of love and care. I was part of something big!

When my creature-load came to a rather large building, he slid off me and handed my rope to those who had led me away from my master. I was led to where my mother was standing. Wow! I could hardly wait to tell her what happened to me. I will never be the same. I will always work hard to do a good job because of what that first burden was to me.

I WAS THERE

As they were going out, they met a man from Cyrene, named Simon, and they forced him to carry the cross.

Matthew 27:32

DESTINY TO SERVE

I was told by my neighbors I began as a seed. I remember how mammoth the world around me appeared from the ground looking up. There were many colorful varieties of my neighbors who were either stately and tall or short and bushy. I eventually outgrew the shorter bushy neighbors around me. As the seasons passed, I could watch the world over the top of my tall stately neighbors. I thought I could see forever.

Strange to me, neighbors of mine would topple over with a thunderous crash to the ground below. The distressing sound of their support fibers separating I will never forget. I could not see what made them fall, but I noticed there were several small moving creatures forcing my neighbors to move out of sight and disappear. Those small creatures made noises I had never heard before. They caused changes I did not understand.

Seasons grew into years, and I delighted in my appearance. I also welcomed new neighbors growing up to my height. I could share the endless scenery. The wind blew in and around us, and we whispered to each other in awe about the magnificent views.

I do not know when it happened or how it took place, yet all the support holding me up gave way. I felt a rush of wind. The world around me flashed by, and I smashed into the ground beneath me where my earlier neighbors had fallen. All so quickly at that moment, I looked at how big the world seemed once more. Everything around me was stately and tall or short and bushy, just like my early years.

I moved over the ground by some force other than what once held me up. A force I could not stop. I do not know how long I was moving, but it seemed a long time. Everything changed around me. I could not see any tall or bushy, short neighbors. More small creatures were moving me around. I was laid on my side with other long neighbors. We just lay together, all close with some on top of others. All was quiet for some time, and I wondered what would happen to me next.

After several days passed, those small creatures appeared and pulled and rolled me away from my neighbors. The sunlight was hot, and I could tell the moisture in me was being drawn out. After a few hot days, two small creatures touched me with something that made me feel I was getting shorter. How strange, I was laid down beside myself in long lengths. One of those lengths was made into even shorter lengths. Everything that I ever remembered about myself being all together disappeared.

The next day, a short part of myself was placed on my long length. I was lifted up and left to lean on neighbors who looked just like me. I felt so unwanted. I was sideways to myself. My short length was across my long length.

What use is this situation for anything? I felt used, abused, naked, and no good for anything.

While I pondered in self-pity what would ever happen to me, two small creatures yanked me from my resting place. I was moved to an open area. One creature, halting and unsteady, picked me up and carried me. I felt the end of my long length dragging on the ground. A little later, that creature dropped me on the hard ground. It was only a moment, but another small creature lifted me again and the dragging continued. There were all kinds of small creatures making noises on every side. Yet I was pulled right through them.

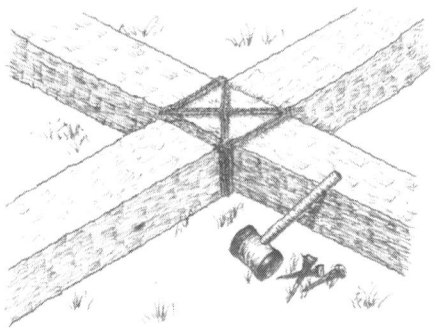

Before long, I was dropped flat down. I was at the mercy of what those small creatures would do. In the next moment, one creature was placed over me, covering both my short and long lengths. There was something from that creature dripping on me. There was a circle of small creatures all around me. I felt the short and long lengths of the creature being attached to me tightly. And there was more dripping on me. It was red. I had never seen that before.

I remember a gentle breeze as I was suddenly pushed up again with the creature fastened to me. There I was, up with small creatures moving around me, making sounds to the creature attached to me. To my amazement, I heard the attached creature make a noise to another small creature. Something that I could understand for the first time: "Today, you will be with me in paradise."

I no longer felt used and abused nor naked and of no use. I felt at one with that creature, serving some kind of mutual purpose for which I did not understand before. The sky became dark. When light began to come back, the creature on me was pulled off and carried away. I was alone yet not alone. Something special happened to me. I hope and wait for that creature to come to me again. I will wait in hope, no matter how long it takes or what happens to me.

PART TWO

GOD'S VOICE IN THE PRESENT

"I believe that I cannot by my own reason or strength believe in Jesus Christ, my Lord, or come to him; but the Holy Spirit has called me by the gospel, enlightened me with his gifts, sanctified and kept me in the true faith."

Martin Luther

SEQUA

The five previous stories bear witness to an event when God's Word was present. What about today? Is God's Word still speaking? With all of today's technology inserted into our ears and displayed for our eyes to see with TV's, headsets, earphones, computers, iPads and iPods, and now the iCloud, etc., I will condense all this electronic mass into one word, fog.

Let us take a reflective journey and ask you, the reader, to answer the questions for yourself.

THE CLOCK STOP WATCHER

When your life begins to look like you are driving through thick fog, time becomes an ally or enemy.
Either you cannot be seen or what you want to see or do is for naught.
Time permits questions to emerge from the fog in your brain.
Questions seek answers, and that takes time.
Questions press through your fog for solutions.
Some solutions are easily perceived.
Other solutions are never realized until disaster arrives.
Have you ever reached that moment of asking, "What is my purpose? Why am I here now, in this age, time and place?

But, first, allow me to ask you these questions. Whose purpose was it in the first place to even allow for your conception? Who started your first heart beat as like a stop watch begins to time your life? There was no time set aside for you to evolve. You became an original, authentic being with the consent of the "Yes!"

I WAS THERE

Who chose the time for you to emerge and take your first breath? What forces were at play in the fog of your learning? Whose purpose drives your life through the fog of time? Permit me to offer an insight to the list of answers for what, or whom, you seek.

There is His power so divine, so majestic, so powerful that did give His "Yes, it's time!" to you to begin living a life meant for a purpose. This "Yes" had love encapsulated all around you. You did not see it, feel it, or know it at the time, yet it was there. The world, as you know it, was created from this same majestic and divine power.

"Where in this creation is perfection," you ask? "There is corrosion, friction among people, lies, greed, fires, bloodshed, bullies, just to get started."

"Where in MY purpose for living is there perfection?" Everything I endeavor to do comes up lacking something, wearing out, or being rejected and maybe even destroyed by people's words or action."

Take a breath for a second. What if I give you something (like a key) given to me years ago. This "key" is free and clear from me to you. It is a gift. If you take it, I loose nothing. If you refuse it, I loose nothing. How can I be so generous? It is because this gift is from the One and only One whose very word made all things we know in and around the world.

What I am about to give you is from the One who said, "Yes!", to my existence, (and yours). That power of , "Yes!", that Word spoken that formed you also has a purpose, backed with a promise. That purpose and promise is able to walk with you in the world that you described above, all broken and corruptible. You want a perfect world? So do I. The key to that perfect world is waiting for you to use. Take the key and unlock the words from the Creator of your existence. Those words offer you a plan with a promise that is able to take your broken, imperfect life that you have now and it will show you where the perfect life is and who alone is able to get you there.

"What about dying," you ask? "I feel insecure." At the end of this life there is the perfect life promised to you. The passage through the door called death has no sting. The key opens the way. The key offers forgiveness for any sin. The result of that forgiveness is a clean slate before your Creator.

The One who started your stop watch of life is waiting. Your clock stop watch is ticking. The Clock Stop Watcher is watching, calling, and waiting. He alone knows when your time is up. He alone gives you the faith to use the key.

Time is ticking. Time becomes your ally or enemy. Time allows you to clear the fog in your brain. Your heart beat has a new rhythm, fresh with new life. The Clock Stop Watcher is patient and generous to you. That is His purpose, to invite you to know all about Him and His Son who cleared the way through the fog of this world. His Spirit gives you the ability to comprehend the tremendous sacrifice of God's Son, Jesus Christ, for you to be another original, authentic person destined for Heaven. Jesus' sacrifice was His death for all human kind. He took all the sins ever committed, and to be committed, to Hell for all time. His victory was rising from that kind of death to witness to the world that He has accomplished what we cannot do, that is, save ourselves.

I WAS THERE

So, take the time to use the key. Take time to clear your way through the fog in your life. The Clock Stop Watcher who said "Yes!" when you began life is waiting to say "Yes! " again to a new life when your stop watch stops.

WHERE CAN I GO FROM HERE?

"IN THE SAME WAY HE CALLS, GATHERS, ENLIGHTENS, AND SANCTIFIES THE WHOLE CHRISTIAN CHURCH ON EARTH, AND KEEPS IT WITH JESUS CHRIST IN THE ONE TRUE FAITH.

IN THIS CHRISTIAN CHURCH HE DAILY AND RICHLY FORGIVES ALL MY SINS AND THE SINS OF ALL BELIEVERS.

ON THE LAST DAY HE WILL RAISE ME UP AND ALL THE DEAD, AND GIVE ETERNAL LIFE TO ME AND ALL BELIEVERS IN CHRIST. THIS IS MOST CERTAINLY TRUE."

MARTIN LUTHER

SEQUA

It is possible that by now you recognize a higher power that invites you to be a different and more purposeful individual. In the first sequa above I condensed all electronic media and devices into being a "fog" in your life.

Now at this point, why not consider using this "fog" in your life as an ally? An ally that is able to pursue real answers to questions about your purpose in God's plans.

The following list is merely comprised of stepping stones of thought with Bible references that may just lead you to a solution you seek. This takes trust and time, so take one stepping stone at a time.

1. Forgiveness is the doorstop that keeps Heaven's gate open.   Mark 11:25; Luke 23:34

2. People make decisions - God knows all the alternatives.   Genesis 50:20

3. A measure of really knowing yourself is the degree to which you care for others.   John 3:16; Galatians 5:22-26

4. Have you wondered if God has His own substitute list when you don't show up? Luke 10:30-36

5. There is a phrase God does not use, "I should have done it." Genesis 1 & 2

6. God is changeless. We NEED change to allow growth, imagination and discovery to take place. Luke 2: 40, 52

7. A teacher/parent teaches children when he/she doesn't always know all the answers. They discover. Psalms 89:15; Proverbs 13:20

8. The image of the Church is being pulled together to reach out. Matthew 28:19-20

9. To be really unpredictable, daily do what Christ tells you. Matthew 19:16-30

10. Your thoughts are the company you keep. Proverbs 14:15; Hebrews 4:12-13

11. In your plans for life, did you ask God for His blue prints for you? Romans 8:30; Ephesians 1:4-5

12. God's math has a positive return for every negative encounter. Romans 8:28-39

13. The Holy Spirit knows what tools are best suited for your task. Romans 12

14. The best strides overall are initiated with the shortest steps. Psalm 23

15. You may be run over as a bridge, however, you keep two pathways connected. Romans 10:10-15; Matthew 18:15-20

16. The price of a dream not shared may cost thousands a gift. Proverbs 18:20-21

17. Mission is God's mind over matter. Isaiah 55

18. Not all instruments are meant to be a solo, they add harmony, rhythm, and balance. Romans 12

19. People are more important than mistakes. Romans 12:9-21

20. Are you in God's lost and found box? Luke 15

21. If God gives us a new day each day, why do we hang onto the reruns in life? Isaiah 6:5-8; Romans 12:9

22. God gave man only two processes: the ability to put together or separate. Ecclesiastes 3:1-8

23. Hope is a spiritual bag packed daily and ready for travel. Psalm 42 & 62

24. Buying a gift is external. Giving a gift is internal. Luke 11:11-13

25. Math formulas are for everyone. God's formulas are for each one individually. Matthew 11:11; Acts 2:38-39; I Corinthians 12:12-30

26. Attitude check: obligations in life could become opportunities. Philippians 2:3-16

27. God blesses. The devil maneuvers. II Corinthians 11:13-15; Revelation 20:7-10; John 3:16

28. Love is the strongest, yet most vulnerable ally we have. John 3:16

29. Trust between two people is as strong as the weaker link. Song of Songs

30. Do you love your hands enough to do something for somebody else? Proverbs 31:10-31

31. If all of life were rules, you would not need people. Matthew 15:1-9; 16:1-12

32. People teach about ladders. Jesus teaches about paths. Psalm 23:3; 25:4

33. True wisdom is recognizing God's point of view for you. Proverbs 11:30; James 1:5

34. You can not control the future. You can improve the present. The lesson is in the past. Isaiah 55:8-13

35. When you walk in faith, you trust the Provider, not the provided. Luke 12:22-34

36. As an instrument of God's plan, are you performing the tune He has for you? James 3:1-12

Dear reader, it is my hope that a few seeds have been sown into your life. May they develop into recognizable purposes. The five protagonists from Part One were present when the voice of God was spoken, so that they could declare, "I was there, destined to witness."

As you look back on your life, may that same voice now cause you to declare, "I was there, destined to witness," in your legacy. May the peace of Christ that passes all understanding keep your heart and mind safe until that day when the Clock Stop Watcher welcomes you home.

Psalm 121

I lift up my eyes to the hills - where does my help come from?

My help comes from the Lord, the Maker of Heaven and earth.

He will not let your foot slip - He who watches over you will not slumber; indeed, He who watches over Israel will neither slumber nor sleep.

The Lord watches over you - The Lord is your shade on your right hand; the sun will not harm you by day, nor the moon by night.

The Lord will keep you from all harm - He will watch over your life; the Lord will watch over your coming and going both now and forevermore. (NIV)

ACKNOWLEDGEMENTS

Inside illustrations:
Mervin Munster taught at various Lutheran schools for nearly 43 years, six of those years working with Gary Gable who became a good friend. Mervin is now enjoying retirement, living with Pat, his wife, in Forest Grove, Oregon, where he dabbles in art, a lifelong passion.

Computer technology:
Peter Martin is the sixth-grade teacher and technology director at Zion Lutheran School in Lake Stevens, Washington. He and his wife, Sheila, and son, James, live in Snohomish, Washington. They spend their vacations exploring our National Parks.